The Adventures of the Sizzling Six: The Lone Tree

The Adventures of the Sizzling Six:
The Lone Tree

Claire Datnow

Media Mint Publishing
Birmingham, USA

SECOND MEDIA MINT BOOK EDITION, 2011

For information:
Media Mint Publishing
2021 Brae Trail,
Birmingham, Alabama 35242
www.mediamint.net

Library of Congress Cataloging-in-Publication Data
Datnow, Claire
The Adventures of The Sizzling Six:
The Lone Tree/Claire Datnow
Includes biographical data
1.Claire Datnow
2. Eco Mystery–series–tween–young adult–fiction
3.Tree conservation–white oak
4. YA environmental literature
5. City ordinances protecting trees
6.Environmentalism

LCCN:2011912250
ISBN: 978-0-9842778-0-3
eBook ISBN: 978-0-9842778-2-7

Book and cover design by Boris Datnow

Printed in the United States of America

iv

To my precious granddaughters, Sonia, Emily, Claudia, Madeline, Lilly, and Elise, and to all the children of the Earth.

Enjoy nature with all your heart and all your senses. Cherish and protect all living things. Nature is your friend. You are part of it, and it is part of you.

Acknowledgements

I would like to thank my readers Cleo Lackey, Elizabeth Kohn and Kara Ganter, this book has benefited from their judicious editing and wise insights. Thanks to Madeline for the story of "The Lonely Apple Tree." Also with heartfelt thanks for the constant support and encouragement of my husband, Boris Datnow.

Contents

One

Deep in the Forest

This is just a small story really, about, among other things: six determined teenagers, a cranky neighbor, an unusual teacher, a big bully, his silly girlfriend, a mysterious dreamtime eagle, and a magnificent oak standing alone in a patch of red dirt.

Not so long ago—around the time your great-grandparents were born—the oak grew deep in the middle of a forest surrounded by countless pine, oak, hickory, elm, beech, maple, and sycamore trees.

From the beginning of its life as a tiny acorn dropped by a careless squirrel, the majestic tree lived through more than a hundred winters, a hundred springs, a hundred summers, and a hundred autumns. As the years passed, the oak's trunk grew broader and taller, and its branches spread wider and higher. The oak became a nature preserve for a variety of creatures. Birds sheltered in its branches, and squirrels scampered up its trunk. For some, it provided a home; for others, a hunting ground. In the fall, mice, squirrels, chipmunks, raccoons, skunk, deer, and even black bear feasted on its acorns. The acorns supplied the extra calories these animals needed to survive the winter.

The forest in which the tree grew stretched for miles. No one lived nearby. At night only the moon, the stars and the wind sent silvery shadows dancing across the trees; only the croaking frogs and chirping cicadas played music in the dark.

The four seasons kept on turning like a great rainbow-colored pinwheel; animals gave birth, grew to old age and died, new plants sprang up and matured. Nothing interrupted this cycle of life in the forest—until people with their tools and machines arrived. Then EVERYTHING changed!

A Small Introduction:
Where are my manners? I should introduce myself. You see, I'm the old oak in the story, but I'm embarrassed to tell it using the first person, or I. I sounds a little swollen headed, so I'll just use the third person, or refer to

myself as the oak tree, or Alba. I'm a white oak, not a red or black oak, not a water oak or a live oak, although I'm related to all of them. My Latin name is Quercus alba, of the Fagaceae family. You probably have seen members of my family growing in the woods around your neighborhood. Some of us are ancient. The oldest white oak I knew lived in the forest about five miles west of Highlands, North Carolina. It grew to be 450 years old. We ancient ones have never felt the sharp cut of the axe or the saw. We are the survivors, and we have tales to tell.

Two

Mortaberg Overruns the Forest

A day's journey on foot, far away from the towering oak in the heart of the forest, stood the city of Mortaberg.

Some Noteworthy Facts:
I was just a little sapling when men completed the railroad, 125 years ago, marking the beginning of Mortaberg as a settlement. Centuries before that, Native Americans lived in the area. Mounds have been discovered near Mortaberg containing clay pots and arrowheads, axes and clubs cut from hard flint. Right now I can feel a few sharp arrowheads digging into my roots. Ouch!

Over decades, the small settlement with a few houses and stores, grew into a town then expanded into a city filled with people rushing about, roads choked with careening cars, shopping malls sprawling over the land, parking lots clogged with vehicles, schools and houses leaning close together, and skyscrapers shutting out the sunlight. Mortaberg kept on growing. It spread over the meadows and into the woods, clearing away trees to make room for more buildings and highways—until only a small emerald island surrounded the oak.

Years passed and the oak grew stronger and taller. Nothing disturbed it, nothing changed on the island. Then in just hours the tree was in extreme JEOPARDY!

The danger came without warning. On a peaceful summer morning, as sunbeams darted through the branches, spreading golden puddles on the ground, a loud groaning, tearing noise echoed through the woods, terrifying all the creatures living on the forest island.

Birds stopped singing and huddled down in their nests. Insects stopped flitting around flowers and vanished under leaves. Squirrels and chipmunks, mice and snakes quit hunting for food and scurried into their burrows. The fearful din went on all through the day. Only when the sun swam low in the sky trailing long, purple shadows over the ground, did the animals, quivering with fear, dare to emerge from their hideouts to find water and food.

6

The next day, the horrible noise started again. It grew louder and louder, closer and closer to the great oak—until a yellow monster came crashing through the trees, filling the air with the raw smell of broken tree limbs, and with suffocating red dust. The birds, the insects, the animals, all froze before exploding into action. Out of every tree and bush, out of the earth and air, living creatures burst forth. Everything that could move wriggled, crawled, slithered, ran, or flew away in panic. Unable to understand what was happening they fled for their lives.

The monster machine struck again and again, and with every fallen tree decades went down. All day the bulldozer hacked into the forest, downing trees with blood-chilling groans and mighty crashes that made the earth tremble.

Only the venerable oak remained rooted firmly to the ground as the bulldozer's greedy steel jaws roared nearer and nearer. The monster machine kept on coming, churning dust clouds around the tree, catapulting sharp sticks and stones into its trunk. Nearer and nearer the machine rumbled until its sharp blades scraped the very ends of the oak's roots, making its branches tremble and sending a nest with six blue eggs smashing to the ground.

As the bulldozer lifted its maw into the air ready to bite, black clouds began gathering rapidly overhead; lightning sparked, thunder snarled, the wind howled. Within minutes, the fury of the storm broke. Rain came down in sharp splinters, ripping leaves off the oak, bending its limbs to the ground, and churning the dirt into chocolate pudding.

When the tempest died away, night, like the inside of an upturned witch's cauldron, concealed the destruction. Not a living thing moved; not a robin, not a squirrel, not even a beetle or an ant. The forest island had been wiped out, replaced by toppled trees, cracked earth, torn roots and upturned boulders. In the midst of this ruin the ancient oak still stood tall. But for the first time in its life, lights from nearby houses and the headlights of cars penetrated the darkness around it.

A Small Confession:
I was afraid, very afraid. Even a great tree cannot survive the attack of humans and their machines.

Three

After the Storm

The day after the storm, the bulldozer's driver returned, wearing heavy lace-up boots and a lopsided grimace on his face. He jumped into the seat, took hold of the steering wheel, and started the machine with a roar. The bulldozer's huge tires spun around and around, digging deeper into the muck. He wedged fallen logs under the tires, but it didn't help. With an angry snort, the driver jumped down and stomped away, mud dripping from his boots and his pants.

The following morning, Sarah Datdan, a teenager with long, dark brown hair, and dreamy hazel eyes, came to the lone oak tree with her dad. Craning her neck far back, she searched for the top of the tree. Its hefty trunk rose upward, like the mainmast of an immense sailing ship, supporting wide spreading branches, reaching into the sky. Sarah stood gazing upward, listening to the wind play haunting melodies above their heads, watching banners of golden sunlight ripple through the leaves, turning each one into a jade-green jewel.

"Wow!" Sarah exclaimed, her voice spiraling into the air.

Smiling at the wonder of the mighty lone tree, Sarah plucked her fingers tentatively along its rough grey trunk, enjoying the soft grainy sound her fingernails made. She stroked its bark again, this time slowly with the palm of her hand. It felt like magic, like beauty.

Turning to her dad with a frown, Sarah asked, "What happened to all the other trees?"

"I'm planning to build my office here," he explained. "The bulldozer cleared the woods to make way for it."

"Oh, Dad, please don't let the bulldozer take this one last tree down! You have to save it!"

"This really is a grand old tree, but . . ." he broke off, and looked thoughtful.

Sarah held her breath, waiting for her dad to finish his sentence. The breeze stopped rustling in the leaves, and in the silence the oak seemed to be listening.

"I just can't promise to save it."

Sarah's shoulders sagged. "Please, Dad, you have to think of something!"

"Okay, I'll try to come up with a plan."

"Really?" she squawked.

He nodded.

"Thanks Dad! I'll bring my friends to see it," she exclaimed, throwing her arms around him.

"Don't get your hopes too high," he warned his daughter.

A few words from Sarah:
Our adventure started with my father ordering the little islands of woods to be scraped away— because of that my friends and I learned some very valuable lessons.

Four

The Sizzling Six Discover the Oak

The oak remained standing alone, the only tree for miles around. Sarah, who lived in the neighborhood nearby, rode by the tree on her bicycle to and from school. It didn't look as if it belonged there now, solitary, abandoned, surrounded by blocks of brick houses.

Some Facts About Sarah:
She is a dreamer
She has a vivid imagination
She adores Rosie her tortoise shell cat

On the first day of summer vacation, she

brought her special friends, Clara, Alex, Rose, Sophie, and Grace to visit the lone oak.

When Alex saw it, she spread her arms wide and cried, "Wow, it's huge! It's beautiful!"

Putting her hands on her hips, Grace exclaimed indignantly, "Why in the world did they smash down the forest that surrounded this wonderful tree?"

"My Dad says he's really sorry he didn't think about saving more trees before putting up his building." Sarah could feel her cheeks blushing red with embarrassment.

"We have to make sure no one ever harms it," Sophie said, her deep-set, dark eyes flashing.

The girls stood in a half circle around the tree, shoulders touching. From behind a lonely cloud, the sun dripped yellow light onto the oak; it glowed on the pure green leaves, and shone on the inky feathers of a crow cawing on a branch. The wind tickled their noses and whispered in their ears, a torn newspaper flapped by, and the loud offensive sound of a motorbike startled them out of the peaceful spell.

A Small Observation:
People rarely take time to notice the ever-changing kaleidoscope of sights, smells, colors and sounds around them—they are too busy rushing around. They should, because it's so interesting.

"This is the perfect place for a hangout,"

Grace said.

"You mean like a private space to meet with our friends?" Sophie asked.

"Yeah, sort of like a teen club."

They tested Grace's idea in their heads, tasting it like a piece of candy just popped into each of their mouths.

Then Rose shouted, "That's great!"

"Let's give ourselves a name," Alex suggested.

The girls looked thoughtful, considering all the possibilities.

"How about Nature Girls Six?" Grace said.

"We need something more exciting," Alex said.

"How about we call ourselves The Sizzling Six," Rose shouted.

They looked at one another.

"I like it!" Clara declared.

"Okay, then who votes yes?" Sarah asked.

They all raised their hand, except Grace. "I liked my name better."

"Well, we used the word six, so it's partly your idea," Clara pointed out.

Grace made a face but agreed with a sigh, "All right then."

With that settled, they all high fived their approval.

"Shouldn't we hold a meeting at this tree to talk about ideas for our club?" Alex asked, itching to get started.

"The ground is covered in thorny weeds and lots of rocks. We should bring blankets from home," Clara, always the practical one, suggested.

"Good idea," Sophie agreed.

"I can't wait, our tree seems so lonely," Alex said, feeling the excitement fizz like ice-cold soda pop inside her.

"I want to climb to the top," Rose declared, tossing her curly auburn hair away from her face.

Before anyone could say another word, she scrambled up the lowest limb just within reach. Gripping her hands around it, she hung for an instant, her feet inches above the ground then swung upward. Moving her hands to the next limb, she worked her feet against the bark. A gust of wind made the branches creak and sway, but she kept climbing. Carefully scooting over to a notch between two limbs, she steadied herself and looked down.

"I can see for miles!" she sang out triumphantly, although her heart was pounding, there was a smile on her lips.

Rose's voice came floating down to her friends—standing below with their mouths open—sounding further away than expected.

"Come down!" Clara called.

Rose locked her fingers tightly around a nearby limb, and lowered herself. Up and out she swung. *Swish*, sang the leaves, as they brushed against her skin. *Swash,* replied her jeans as they rubbed against the bark. Suddenly the oak seemed to vibrate with a magnetic force that robbed her body of movement and pulled her hard against a fork in a branch. Rose sat very still, her chest heaving, her ears ringing. When her breathing slowed she scrambled downward. Just before jumping to the ground, she hooked her legs over a limb and hung upside down like an acrobat.

"Dare you to climb as high as I did!" she challenged her friends. Her face itched from the cobwebs brushing across it, and one eye leaked from a small twig flicking across her eyelid, but she wasn't going to tell.

"You're all chicken!" she exclaimed, landing on the ground with a light thud.

Still no one volunteered to take her up on the dare.

As they trudged home for lunch, their heads filled with visions of new and mysterious adventures, the Sizzling Six enthusiastically discussed what they needed to do to launch their club.

Some Facts About Rose:
She is a daredevil
She is very dramatic
She is confident

"I'll make a list of things to do and e-mail it to all of you," Clara volunteered.

"It's going to be so much fun!" Alex exclaimed.

"Why don't we meet early tomorrow morning? It'll be sort of our secret," Sophie, an early riser, suggested.

16

"That's cool," Rose agreed, her eyes shining with anticipation.

"Okay, then. Let's meet at 5:30 outside the firehouse," Sophie said. The other girls agreed, although they hoped they wouldn't be too sleepy to get up in time.

A Realization:
That summer was an ending, and a new beginning. When I look back, I remember with longing the deep old forest surrounding me, now gone forever, but I cherish the start of my friendship with the girls and boys of the neighborhood.

Five

A Great Idea

When the Sizzling Six gathered at the firehouse at daybreak, one pale star still strayed sleepily in the morning sky. As the friends set forth, carrying old blankets and a cooler between them, no one in the neighborhood seemed awake, not even Clara's rooster or ornery Mr. Prickles who went jogging at the crack of dawn. They didn't like him because he chased kids away when they plucked ripe apples off his tree, from branches dangling over the sidewalk; he refused to share although he left his apples to rot on the ground.

Usually the girls chattered away, but it

seemed rude to disturb the quiet of the morning. As they walked, they made footprints in the dew glistening on the grass, listened to birds serenading one another, bees buzzing in the wildflowers, and gingerly touched sticky snails' trails on the leaves.

They spread their blankets under the oak and lay on their backs looking up through its leafy branches to the fresh morning sky. Still half dreaming, Rose gazed up at clouds bobbing about and bumping into each other, like a flock of wooly orange sheep.

"Hey, can you guess what I see in the clouds?" Rose asked.

"A giant yawning?" Alex guessed.

"A Martian space ship?" Clara said.

"An elephant fish with a mouth that looks like a long trunk," Sophie ventured, tracing the outline of the cloud with her index finger.

"There's no such thing," Clara challenged her.

"Yes, there is too, in Australia. I saw them on YouTube," Alex said.

"A huge sandcastle!" Grace shouted.

"Nope, they're sheep," Rose smirked.

Dry mouthed and early-morning hungry, they quit their game to eat sandwiches and drink milk from the cooler.

Some Facts About Alex:
She loves to read
She is thoughtful
She is enthusiastic

"I found out that our tree is a white oak, or *Quercus alba*, that's its Latin name." Alex showed them the illustration in her field guidebook then pointed to the tree and its leaves. "It's straight and tall with wide spreading branches. Its bark is thick and gray and broken into plates like scales. Its leaves have seven to nine rounded lobes, or fingers. See?"

The girls compared the illustration on the page to a leaf that had fallen, and then nodded.

"Hey, why don't we vote to name our tree Quercus Alb*a*?" Alex suggested.

"That's too long," Rose objected.

"How about Maizie?" Grace laughed.

"Hmm . . . maybe just Alba would be good?" Clara said.

"Let's vote," Sophie said.

All voted for Alba, except for Grace—again. She wanted the oak to be named Maizie because it was Amazing.

"Don't pout, Grace. How about we call our tree Maizie Alba, or Alba Maizie, that would be fair wouldn't it?" Sophie said.

"Okay, Alba Maizie sounds fine," Grace conceded. She grinned and lifting her hand in the air, touched her thumb with her index and middle fingers to make a circle of approval.

Some Facts About Grace:
She doesn't like to lose
She marches to her own drum
She has a great sense of humor

Breakfast over, it didn't take long before the hot sun, the spiky weeds, the biting insects, and the hard stones beneath the blanket began to bother them. They all started complaining.

"Maybe this isn't the best place for our club," Sophie said, scratching at an insect bite.

"Aw, don't be such a wuss!" Rose said.

"Hey, be fair! I'm not the only one complaining," Sophie retorted.

"Sophie is right. Let's brainstorm ideas," Clara said.

"Hmm, what about a tent?" Alex asked.

"Maybe we could build a tree house," Sarah suggested, her imagination exploding inside her.

"Yes, really high up where we could see for miles!" Rose's hazel eyes shone with anticipation.

"That would be great!" Grace agreed with a mischievous smile.

"How would we get up there?" Alex asked.

"We could use a rope ladder," Sophie proposed.

"Let's not do anything dangerous," Clara cautioned.

"We should draw up a plan for our tree house. We could look on the Internet for creative ideas," Grace said.

"Yeah, we could build it to look like a space ship, or a medieval castle, maybe even a submarine," Sarah fantasized.

"Whatever we decide, we shouldn't do anything to hurt Alba. Our tree is sad enough already," Sophie patted the tree's trunk gently.

"I agree. But we will need help to build the tree house," Alex pointed out.

"First, I'll have to get my Dad's permission to build it on his property," Sarah reminded them.

"You've got to convince him, because we really want that tree house!" Grace said with a determined look in her eyes.

Some Facts About Sophie:
She is very sensitive
She loves to write stories
She appreciates fairness

Six

Good News, Bad News

Getting Mr. Datdan's consent turned out to be much trickier than the Sizzling Six had anticipated. He explained that to save the tree he would first have to get permission from the Mortaberg City Council to move his building closer to the road.

"What's it got to do with the city council?" Sarah wanted to know.

"It's complicated. You see, there are rules and regulations about how close a building can be to the street," her dad explained.

"How come?"

"It seems that if I move the building

forward, the city will have to move the storm drain, and that will cost a bundle."

"Dad, you can't go back on your promise to save the tree!"

Mr. Datdan sighed, "I'll try not to, but it won't be easy, especially from the chairman of the city council, Mr. Prickles. He watches every last cent the council spends of our tax dollars."

Sarah called Alex on the cell phone and told her the bad news. The two girls talked about what they could do about it.

"We should ask our dads, moms and our neighbors for help," Alex suggested.

"That's a good idea. But in the meantime what about our tree house?"

"We shouldn't give up on it."

"Then what can we do?" Sarah asked.

"First, we should collect money to pay for building supplies for the tree house."

"Okay, Alex. Do you want to call Clara and Rose, and I'll call Sophie and Grace?"

"Okay. Let's meet tomorrow to talk."

The next day, sheltering in Alba's shade, the girls discussed their plans.

"First, how can we get our dads to help us build the tree house—*if* the city council lets my dad move his building?" Sarah asked.

"I've been thinking about that. We should make offers our dads can't refuse. Don't you know if you want to get something you have to give something in return?" Sophie challenged her friends.

24

"Okay, so what will you give your dad?" Rose wanted to know.

"I'll offer to do extra chores to earn the money for supplies to build the tree house. I know my dad needs help weeding his vegetable garden. You all think of something your dad really needs help with, something that he will pay you to do."

"Sophie, your idea's good, but I wish it wasn't going to be so much work!" Grace groaned.

"Well, if you think of something better, let us know!" Alex flashed a fake smile at her.

"Okay, keep your cool," Clara said, nudging Grace with her elbow.

"Let's get together the day after tomorrow. It's Wednesday, so we can meet on Friday," Alex said.

A Noteworthy Note:
I was proud of the way the Sizzling Six were determined to pursue their goal. I didn't want to think about what would happen to me; if they didn't succeed I could end up as firewood.

It rained heavily Friday morning, so the girls had to wait until after lunch. They gathered under Alba late in the afternoon to share their good news—their fathers had agreed to help them in exchange for chores.

"I know we are all excited about the tree house, but what if Sarah's Dad really can't get permission from the council?" Clara asked, the corners of her mouth pulling downward.

Just the thought of that happening made the girls so miserable no one could think of anything to say.

Then Sarah broke the gloomy mood, "Please, can we just put that out of our minds for now?"

"Yes, let's be optimistic," Rose agreed.

"Sarah and Rose are right, we should go ahead with our plans so we'll be ready," Alex agreed.

Now everyone started talking at once about how they wanted the tree house to look.

Over the next few days the girls got busy designing their dream tree house. Some ideas had to be discarded as they were not safe, too expensive, or impractical. In the end, the girls agreed that a platform on stilts would be best; in that way they wouldn't damage the oak by knocking nails into it.

Clara found software that she could use to make a blueprint of their tree house. It took much longer to do the drawing of the plan than she had anticipated, but in the end the praise from her friends was worth the effort.

The Sizzling Six spent the following four weeks working at their chores to earn enough money between them. It took a great deal of hard work. Unfortunately, after attending two council meetings, Mr. Datdan *still* had not received the permission he needed. Sarah couldn't believe that a handful of men and women on the council could seal Alba's fate.

"It seems so wrong that a few adults can decide if a tree should live or die," Sophie commiserated with her friends.

Relaxing on folding chairs beneath Alba, the girls nodded glumly.

"Our city should protect Alba," Sophie declared.

"Not just our tree, but also our forests," Clara added.

"And our rivers and streams, too," Rose kept on.

"There should be a law to protect them!" Grace's eyes flashed, "Like making them plant a new tree for everyone they cut down."

They nodded glumly.

"Maybe there is a law," Sophie said.

"Hey, you could be right!" Grace exclaimed. "Alex, your dad's a lawyer, can he find out of if there really is one?"

"That's a fantastic idea! I'll ask my Dad to check it out, and let you know what he says."

After a few days of waiting anxiously, Alex's father, Mr. Kohn, brought her some interesting news.

"Mortaberg does have a tree conservation ordinance." Seeing the puzzled expression on his daughter's face, he added, "That means there are laws to preserve trees and prevent all of them from being cut down to build houses, offices, and roads."

"Can this ordinance save our tree?"

"I don't know for sure. Let me talk to

Sarah's father. Maybe we can work out a plan to put before the council."

"You're the best!" Alex exclaimed, hugging him. "My friends will be counting on you."

"Don't get your hopes too high, Alex."

Another Noteworthy Note:
The Sizzling Six held a meeting beneath my branches to come up with a plan to get the city council to save me. Grace thought they should call the mayor of Mortaberg and just beg him to rescue me; Rose wanted to go down to city hall, look the mayor in the eye, and tell him what they thought. They debated their ideas long and hard. Finally, they decided to spread the word all around the neighborhood and ask for support. I sure hoped that it would work!

Seven

Showdown with the City Council

At the next meeting of the council, the Sizzling Six and the supporters they had drummed up—fathers, mothers, brothers, grandmothers, grandfathers, neighbors and friends—seated themselves in the council chamber ready to present their plan to save Alba.

"Hope the meeting's not long and boring," Grace whispered in Rose's ear.

"Trust me, it will be, until they get to the part about saving Alba—and our little surprises," Rose whispered back.

And it was boring. When Mr. Kohn finally got up to speak, the girls who had almost dozed off despite the hard wooden seats, sat up and paid attention. He used legal terms they didn't understand, but they got the part about the tree conservation ordinance requiring owners to save a certain number of the trees on a lot during construction. When Mr. Kohn sat down, the girls wanted to rush over and hug him, and the boys wanted to shake his hand, but they would have to wait until the meeting ended.

Sarah's father spoke next. Pointing to the teenagers, he said, "We need to follow the rules set out in our tree conservation ordinance to save trees for our neighborhood, to keep our environment healthy, and for young people like them to enjoy and to learn to appreciate nature."

There followed a boring debate about the expense to the city of moving the storm drains. Mr. Prickles, their grumpy neighbor and chairman on the city council, kept on objecting to spending money.

"We need to be more responsible. We can't spend money on just one tree." Noticing the red faces of the six girls glaring at him, he added, "I have nothing against trees! But I don't have anything against money either, do you?"

The girls looked at each other anxiously; they were sure now that the council would refuse Mr. Datdan's request. With a nasty sinking feeling, they thought about how Alba would soon be chopped down and turned into nothing but kindling.

Next on the agenda, Sophie was called before the council. She started to read her story—one of the girls' surprises—about two trees felled in a storm, but she could feel her knees trembling and hear her voice getting high and squeaky.

When Mr. Prickles called out, "Speak up!" she started stuttering, her words come out in slow motion as of she were talking underwater. She could feel everyone staring at her, especially cranky Mr. Prickles. Out of the corner of her eye she saw her friends gazing at her; they were counting on her, rooting for her. Sophie swallowed hard and started over.

With each sentence her voice grew louder and more confident because she really believed in what she was saying, and wanted to convince the council. When Sophie had finished the Sizzling Six clapped wildly. Surprisingly, members of the council began clapping too, and soon others joined in—all except Mr. Prickles.

Her checks flushed with triumph, Sophie returned to her seat.

A Small Note:
I heard Sophie reading her story aloud, hidden in the tree house beneath my branches. It is a good story. Don't be impatient; you'll get to read it later.

Next Rose stood up—their next surprise.

Although her heart was hammering in her chest, she looked bravely at the members of the city council and asked, "Does the death of one eighty-foot tall, one-hundred-twenty five-year old, healthy oak matter? I know that we'd all be sad and angry to see it killed. I know that an important part of our neighborhood will be gone forever if that oak is chopped down."

Everyone cheered and shouted, "Bravo!" This time the chairman banged his gavel, ordering them to be silent.

After that a second-grader from the elementary school, Sam Minstrel, read his story, "The Lonely Apple Tree." The neighborhood folks were so proud of him.

Once upon a time there was a little Apple tree. It lived in the middle of nowhere. It was very lonely. His only friend was a rock, just a single rock. A few days later a little chipmunk moved in. It brought all of his nuts into the tree. The tree was so happy. One day a family came for a picnic. Now the tree was *super* happy. Soon a boy named Jack and a girl named Jill came wandering up the hill. "Hey!" Jill said, "We've made it up the hill." A few minutes later they went tumbling down. The next season came. A few weeks later 200 flowers bloomed. The tree was *soo* happy. He felt a million times better.

Now it was up to the council to vote for or against Mr. Datdan's request. Would they stand by Mortaberg's law for tree conservation or would they decide to ignore it? They conferred with one another for what seemed like hours, but it was only minutes.

Then the Chairman Prickles looked over his glasses and said slowly and deliberately, "Mr. Datdan due to the cost of moving the storm drains," he paused, reached for a glass of water, took a few sips, cleared his throat then finally declared, "we cannot grant you permission."

The Sizzling Six couldn't stop the tears pooling in their eyes. The boys clenched their fists and muttered so that they could barely be heard, "Dang," and "Gosh Darn," and other not so polite words, before their parents stopped them with angry looks.

The girls stared at Mr. Prickles. No one moved, no one said a word. In the hush they could hear the purr of the air conditioning, the muffled thud of heavy footsteps in the hallway. Slowly, as if in a trance, Sarah turned to look at her dad with big, pleading eyes. Her Dad met her gaze, and then as if an unspoken message had passed between them, he unfolded his long frame and stood up.

"I ask permission to speak," he said calmly, although there was an angry gleam in his eyes. Mr. Prickles frowned, opened his mouth, and then shut it. When he closed and opened his mouth, yet again, a funny thought popped into Grace's head: Mr. Prickles looked hilarious, like a hungry guppy searching for food in an aquarium.

Grace struggled to stop the strange gurgling noises caming out of her mouth and her shoulders from shaking. For a minute her friends thought she was choking, but when she burst out laughing they realized she was having a giggling fit. They tried to control themselves, but they started giggling too. Everyone turned to stare at them, but they couldn't stop.

Only when Mr. Prickles kept on banging his gavel, really hard, did they get control of themselves. Looking at his watch, Mr. Prickles told Mr. Datdan, "You have exactly two minutes to speak!"

In a final desperate attempt to save Alba, Mr. Datdan stepped forward and said, "I will agree to pay part of the cost of the storm drains myself."

People rose to their feet cheering. Once more Mr. Prickles had to bring everyone to order, warning them that they would have to leave if they didn't behave themselves.

The girls held their breath while the council put it to the vote, for the second time. When Mr. Prickles, with a sour look on his face, announced that the majority had voted "yes," the girls rushed forward to hug Mr. Datdan and Mr. Kohn. Even old curmudgeon Mr. Prickles could not prevent them from exchanging grins as wide as a Jack O'Lanterns.

Eight

The Tree House

On the Saturday immediately following the Sizzling Six's triumph at the council, fathers and mothers, big brothers and sisters hauled lumber, nails and tools to Alba. They had no time to lose! They needed every one's help. Only a month remained before the summer vacation was over.

First, they anchored four sturdy wooden posts into the ground with cement. After the cement dried and the poles were firmly anchored, they all helped build a wooden deck over the posts. For safety, around the edges of the rectangular deck they nailed wooden rails about four feet high. It took three weekends of hard work to complete building their house.

Grace's Words:
I remember my blistered hands, the sweat soaking my clothes, the too loud sound of hammering in my ears. But joking with my friends, hearing their laughter is what I remember the best. They kept me going when I all I wanted to do was take a cool shower and veg out in front of the TV.

When their tree house was finally ready, the Sizzling Six scrambled up the rope ladder looped over one of Alba's sturdy branches. They climbed into their tree house feeling as thrilled as if they had won a gold medal at the Olympics. They made the platform cozy with blankets and pillows of waterproof material, and settled back to savor their special place.

The breeze blew through gaps between the planks, keeping them cool in the August heat. Alba's constant motion, around and above them, felt as if they were riding the waves aboard a sailing ship. Hidden in the tree, they lay on their backs and looked up through the floating, moving shade, shifting with the light filtering through the leaves. On an outer branch they spied a mother robin feeding three nestlings from a worm wriggling in her bill, while nearby an agitated mockingbird hopped from limb to limb. As the wind picked up, the chatter of leaves grew louder, and the ripe summer smells floated through the air.

The girls felt the living presence of the tree, massive, strong, sheltering, nourished by the sun and rain for many seasons before their grandfathers and grandmothers were born. Alex whispered, "The Lakota Indians call trees the 'standing people'."

"Being so close to Alba makes me feel as if I can talk to her," Sarah said.

For the rest of summer the Sizzling Six rested in their tree house, talking and dreaming until the clouds turned to tangerine, scarlet and gold at dusk. One night, just a week before the start of school, the Sizzling Six got permission—with some begging—to sleep out under the stars.

Nine

Overnight in the Tree House

By the light of a full moon, the Sizzling Six climbed the rope ladder into the tree house, hauling their sleeping bags, flashlights, drinks, and snacks. Sarah had brought her cell phone so she could call home if they needed help. Excited and nervous about sleeping outside in the mysterious darkness, they kept on talking and joking.

Sophie's Words:
When I look back I remember how the black night was so scary. I really wanted to run back

to the safety of my house, my bed, and my parents. I'm so glad that I didn't.

In intervals of quiet they heard the mysterious murmuring of the leaves, the strange creaking of the branches, the furtive rustling of nocturnal creatures. Grace reached out and touched the rough, scaly bark of Alba Maizie's trunk, and sniffed the faint odor of boiled tealeaves it gave off. In the distance a dog barked a harsh warning, and the delicious spicy smell of barbeque curled through the air. A honey-colored moon, big and round as a beach ball, hung like a cutout decoration stitched onto a black velvet shawl studded with diamonds.

The hours passed slowly. The moon, sailing across the sky from east to west, cast eerie shadows on the ground, and brushed amber sand over the leaves and into their hair. It was close to midnight, but they were still too jumpy to sleep.

"When I was little, I imagined that I was a witch, and could make myself invisible by drinking a glass of milk a certain way," Sophie confided.

"I made believe that I was a famous singer that won all the awards," Grace said.

"I did too! But now I mostly use my creativity on the computer," Clara said.

They gazed up into the firmament, fishing for the starry constellations with their eyes. Lulled by the electric chirring of crickets, and the melodic trill of male tree frogs calling for mates in the summer heat, before they knew it, their eyes closed.

Sarah could not be sure how long she had slept, but it must have been several hours, because when she opened her eyes, the moon hung thin and low on the western horizon. She grabbed her flashlight and was about to switch it on, when a deep triple hoot, *who-who-ah-whoo, who-ah-whoo, who-ah-whoo,* echoed through Alba. Her hair stood up on the back of her neck, and her heart started to race. She stared up into the branches, hardly daring to breathe.

When her eyes adjusted to the dimness, she could make out the shape of a large bird. It wore a downy coat of brown and white feathers, two tufts stuck out of the top of its head like feathery horns, a white collar circled its throat, and a white mask framed its glowing yellow eyes.

The owl looked back at her with its ear tufts standing straight up, and, opening its hooked beak, hooted her name*: Sar-ah, Sar-ah.*

In a weird voice that seemed to come from deep inside her, Sarah answered: *Ow-ow-owl.* And the bird replied. She and the owl repeated their calls to one another five times: *Sa-rah. Ow-ow-owl. Sa-rah. Ow-ow-owl. Sa-rah. Ow-ow-owl. Sa-rah. Ow-ow-owl. Sa-rah. Ow-ow-owl.*

Then the great wise bird spread its wings and flew up through the branches, and as it did so, Sarah rose up into the air like a leaf caught on the wind, until she was looking down on Alba far below her. Then she wheeled in a circle and followed the owl winging silently away.

Ten

Flying through Dreamtime

Sarah and the owl flew over the neighborhood where streetlights twinkled their greetings. They zoomed above church spires, skyscrapers, bridges, and highways scrawling across the land.

When Sarah saw a high building coming toward her, she tried to avoid it by kicking her legs and flapping her arms wildly, but she bumped right into it. Then she noticed how the owl glided smoothly on the currents of air, so she stopped thrashing about, stretched her body flat, and let the airstream lift her upward.

They soared on, leaving behind houses and schools, cars and trucks, noise and lights, factories and smoke, malls and parking lots, and the familiar city smells of sizzling French fries and hamburgers, hot tar and gasoline. On the very edge of Mortaberg they crossed railroad tracks, twisting like silver snakes in the moonlight, and drifted above farmland.

By the light of five scarlet moons floating eerily, crazily in the sky like newborn planets, Sarah spied a farmhouse with a tin roof and a crumbling chimney at each end. Neat rows of corn and beans surrounded the house. A big, hairy black dog with one huge eye looked up and howled at the strange white blur she made in the sky. The vegetable fields gave way to cotton patches then to wild blackberry bushes, deep rain gullies, and red clay hills followed by to young pines, growing where the deep forests had been slashed and burned.

Sarah could not tell how many times the sun and the five strange moons rose and fell as she zoomed back deep into the past. Alone with the owl, she rode the night wind above ancient forests devoid of people. They flew on and on until she grew very sleepy, but whenever she shut her eyes, she began tumbling to earth and awoke with a terrible shudder.

As another day dawned, Sarah's body grew too heavy to move. She could not keep her eyes open for another second.

She began falling, head over heels, down and down, faster and faster. Feeling certain that she would crash and crack her skull against a rock, she opened her mouth to scream but it stuck in her throat like a giant thorn.

She tried to wake herself, but she couldn't. She kept on spinning downward, until she was flopping around like a fish out of water, gasping for air. As she was about to smash into the mountain, the owl dived below her and she hurtled into him with a great *thwack*! The bird gave a terrible screech and feathers flew everywhere—but the impact stopped her fall. Trembling with relief, she followed the owl as it spiraled downward to perch on a boulder at the edge of a canyon.

For a long time, Sarah rested beside the owl, panting and shaking. Venus, the dazzling morning star, shone low in the east. A chorus of birds sang of love—*where are you?* And war—*stay away from my territory*! Between pearly ribbons of morning mist, Sarah caught the green glint of a river zigzagging through the canyon far below. They stayed there, sucking dew from the leaves and honey from wildflowers, until the sun burned the mist away.

When the owl hooted and spread its great wings, Sarah knew it was time to continue their journey. She flapped her arms as hard as she could, but rose very slowly as if swimming in a lake of molasses. She yelled for the owl to wait, but he ignored her cries.

As Sarah trailed behind the owl, she looked

down on a forest so deep it appeared to be a velvet quilt stitched together with a thousand multihued patches of green. She could see no signs of human beings, only trees and sky stretching away to the horizon. Suddenly, a giant tree tumbled to earth with a scary whooshing, groaning sound, and lay quivering with its roots in the air. In the gap made by the fallen tree, Sarah saw people moving busily below like miniature figurines.

She slowed the beating of her arms and descended to take a closer look. From the stone axes they used to chop down the tree, and the animal skins they wore she guessed that they were Native Americans.

She kept winging on through dreamtime back toward the present. Suddenly, the forest twitched like the hide of a sleeping dog when a million fleas are biting. More people poured into the woods, on foot, on horseback, in wagons loaded with furniture and beds, and kids huddled together, and fathers holding the reins and a whip, and mothers hunched on wagon seats with poke bonnets on their heads. Wherever they settled, villages and towns sprang up, ripping the forest into shreds and patches.

Sarah longed to return to her friends in the tree house, but she didn't know how to find her way home; she had to keep on flying with the owl.

Now they were zooming faster and faster. The wind in her ears whistled like waves crashing on shore. Suddenly, the owl pressed its ear tufts flat against its head and it hooted out an alarm call. Above the howling wind she heard the bone-rattling roar of machines. Looking down, Sarah saw an army of bulldozers hacking at the woods. Wherever the bulldozer cleared the trees, modern houses, skyscrapers, shopping malls, and highways sprang up.

Then they were flying over Mortaberg and her neighborhood, circling Alba, at last. A surge of happiness made Sarah laugh out loud. The owl spread its claws, and swiftly, silently swooped down on a mouse scampering away. With one swipe of its sharp, black talons it caught the rodent and swallowed it whole. Satisfied, the great bird blinked its round yellow eyes twice, and then flew off.

Sarah called out, "Come back, Owl! Come back!"

When it was nothing but a speck in the distance, she felt herself falling, and cried out for help. Her friends in the tree house rolled out of their sleeping bags, terrified that something awful had happened. Sarah found herself clinging to a limb above them, feeling as dizzy and weak as if she had been rocketed through space on a time machine.

"What are doing up there? Get down before you fall," Clara called out.

Rose climbed to a nearby branch to help Sarah down. Shakily she descended to the tree house, where she gulped water to quench her thirst. Searching for the right words, Sarah tried to tell her friends about how she flew with the owl back through time, to ancient forests where no man lived, and how she saw the forest being cut down to make way for villages then towns and cities.

"What a fantastic dream!" Grace exclaimed.

"It's sad that people cleared the endless forest away," Sophie said.

"I wish that I had been the one who flew with the owl!" Rose exclaimed.

"Do you think your dream was sending a message to us?" Alex asked.

Sarah closed her eyes and thought hard, then said dreamily, "The wise owl showed me that the spirits of Life are the throbbing sun, the flowing streams, and the trees. The spirits of Truth are the birds singing in the trees, and animals hunting in the forests." To her regret, as she spoke the dream images began to fade away.

On the way home after their amazing night in the tree house, everyone was very quiet, thinking about Sarah's magical dream.

A Little Poetry:
As I listened to Sarah's dream a poem rose inside me like sap flowing up from my roots. May I share it?

47

Locked in life's fierce embrace,
The snake and the owl kill
squirrel and mouse
with ferocious, unappeasable jaws.
The raccoon and the opossum greedily crack
birds' eggs
with sharp teeth and bloody claws.
The sun grows trees
in its life-giving rays.
All living things live freely,
yet tethered to instinct,
to each other and
to time's unstoppable march.

Eleven

Adopting Alba

When school began after the action-packed summer vacation, the girls shared their adventures with their teachers and classmates at Stone Middle School. They told them about Alba, the great lone white oak, and the tree house they had built beneath it.

Mrs. Green, Sarah and Alex's science teacher, thought it would be interesting for her class to adopt the tree just a few blocks away from the school. Mrs. Green was a tiny, energetic woman, with a big voice. When the light caught her hair you could see strands of green glistening in it. The students couldn't tell if she had colored them, if they were hair extensions, or natural—no one had the nerve to ask.

Mrs. Green expected them to be as enthusiastic about exploring and studying nature as she was, and she didn't hesitate to give students poor grades if they failed to do their homework or didn't try their best.

Strange rumors about their teacher circulated around the school. Some said that her husband was a lumberjack up in Alaska, and that she kept a menagerie of injured or abandoned wild animals in her home. Both students and teachers were a little afraid of her, yet they respected her. Mrs. Green's students learned a lot in her class and scored well on tests.

Thanks to Mrs. Green, the idea of adopting Alba as their project spread to the others science teachers, Mr. Birch and Mr. Byrd, and then around the school. They planned on taking field trips to follow the life cycle of the oak, and to observe and photograph the life around it.

As the last days of summer drew to an end, the classes came to visit Alba then made plans for field trips in the fall, the winter and the spring when they could sketch, photograph, make notes and keep journals. Stone Middle teachers also asked their students to write stories about Alba. Did the oak witness the induction of their state to the union? Did it see the last of the Native Americans in their state?

Did their tree observe the pioneers building their new homes and harnessing the power of the natural world around them? How did it come about that Alba was not chopped down for lumber or firewood? The answers were buried deep within its age rings.

Some interesting Facts:
Dendrochronology is the science of tree rings. By studying the rings inside a trunk after it has been cut down, scientists can determine the age of the tree, how fast it grew each year, and what the climatic conditions were like during that year. Tree ring: A layer of wood cells produced by a tree or shrub in one year. This is all very interesting, but I don't look forward to having the inside of me examined any time soon.

By the fall, Alba's acorns had matured into ripe nuts. When the children stood under Alba on a windy day, acorns pelted down on their heads. *Swish!* Acorns sailed aloft into the air. The missiles streaked toward the earth bringing other nuts with them as they fell. *Pop! Smack!* They plopped on the ground like miniature apples. Soon the forest creatures came scurrying out to gobble and to store them. The students were amazed to learn that the chances of one acorn growing into an oak tree are very small—for every 10,000 acorns, only one will become a tree!

A Small Observation:
Many of the students enjoyed adopting me, they especially liked going on field trips. The Sizzling Six did their best to ignore the few students who called them names like "tree huggers."

The Sizzling Six invited their classmates to come after school to observe the wildlife from the tree house. If they stayed very still, they could watch squirrels hiding acorns to last them through the winter when food is scarce; a gray squirrel can bury acorns at the rate of one a minute. Chipmunks, woodpeckers also hunted for acorns, competing with the squirrels for the best ones.

Alba's leaves changed colors, splashing purplish brown across the blue October skies. The birds of summer hurried to fly south as the leaves twirled to earth, some snaring in bushes and spiders' webs. Now a thick skin of leaves covered the acorns so that the animals could not always find them. Many of the buried nuts rotted in the leaf mold and could not be eaten by the creatures that had first hidden them.

One evening, as the sun's last rays slipped down to tickle a swarm of gnats, the six friends sat quietly in the tree house observing life around them; they were rewarded for their patience when a deer and later a wild turkey came to feast on the fallen acorns. The handsome turkey scratched away at the coppery cloak of leaf litter on the ground, cramming his crop with dozens of the nuts. The Sizzling Six captured excellent photos of the visitor, although Clara had to clamp her hand over Rose's mouth to stop her from jumping with excitement and frightening him away.

Some Facts About Clara:
She has excellent common sense
She loves discovering new things on the computer
She enjoys a challenge

Back in class the next day, the teenagers learned that acorns were not only food for animals they were once a staple food for Native Americans. For centuries, they boiled and pounded acorns into coarse flour to make bread, or roasted them to eat as nuts.

Twelve

A Stormy Night

The weekend before Thanksgiving, most of the acorns were gone. Alba's graceful branches were almost bare; the few leaves on the tree rubbed together making the sound of old newspaper flapping in the wind. That Saturday the girls persuaded their parents to allow them to spend just one more night in the tree house before winter set in. The Sizzling Six bundled up in warm clothing and brought along insulated sleeping bags. Bunching together, they munched sandwiches letting the crumbs gather in the folds of their sweaters, inhaling the sweet tang of peanut butter and jam, and sharing the pleasure of laughter.

"If you were a tree, what kind would you be?" Sophie asked,

"A toiletry," Rose joked.

"A cemetery," Sarah said.

"How about a poetry?" Alex chuckled.

"Or a mystery," Clara added.

"Have you heard the one about the deviltry?" Grace laughed.

As they traded jokes, the girls watched Night come striding in to gather long streamers of scarlet and gold under his black cloak, wanting always to be here, together, a part of their tree. It was the best time of their lives.

When they settled into their sleeping bags, Rose wondered aloud, "Do you think you'll have another weird dream, Sarah?"

"Maybe you'll be the one to dream this time," she replied.

"I hope I do," Rose said.

As they snuggled down, it was so quiet they seemed to be the only living creatures on the planet. No crickets or frogs sang their summer symphony. The sneaky raccoon, the furtive mouse, the wily opossum did not come out to find a mate or to scavenge for food.

"It's so quiet I can hear myself breathing," Clara whispered.

"It's kind of exciting, but really creepy," Sophie whispered back.

"Shush! Do you hear something?" Grace asked.

55

The girls froze. Hardly daring to breath they listened . . . a faint rustling came out of the darkness. A nasty creature could be waiting to attack them! A few seconds went by; no one dared move even a finger.

Alex couldn't stand the tension a second longer, she flicked on the flashlight and with trembling hands, played it over the branches.

In the beam of light they saw a small, furry brown creature hanging upside down from the branch above them. Its eyes were bulging black beads, its outer ears were round and covered in black fur, its inner ears were thick and leathery, and its snout stuck out as if were made of black clay. Sophie's felt as if a cord was tightening around her throat, stomach and ribs. She opened her mouth to scream but the cord wouldn't let the sound out. Then Sarah squealed when a tree branch brushed against the side of her head. Alarmed, the creature spread its leathery black wings wide and glided silently away.

"What was that?" Clara's voice sounded hoarse.

"I-I-I think it's an Evening B-B-Bat," Alex stuttered, trying to stay calm although she was shaking.

"A bat?" Rose giggled nervously.

"We learned about Evening Bats in Mrs. Green's science class," Alex said.

"Yeah, we sure did. I remember she told us that they suck human blood," Grace added.

"Oh, No!" Sophie screamed.

"Calm down, she's just kidding," Clara reassured her.

"Those bats usually roost in tree holes, not in caves, and they feed on insects—not people—and therefore are beneficial to humans," Alex explained.

"Wow, whatever it was, it sure scared us!" Sophie said nervously.

"It did, but it's a really cool creature," Rose said.

The fright made it even harder for the Sizzling Six to get to sleep. They huddled together for safety. After a long while they drifted off.

Just before sunrise, they were awakened by the wind whistling loudly in the treetop. Above Alba's swaying branches, ominous thunderheads gathered to cover the moon, mopping away its light.

"Time to race for home!" everyone yelled.

As they dashed to Clara's house just half a block away, Alex tripped over a crack in the sidewalk. Just then they saw Clara's dad running toward them.

"Run to the house," he shouted.

As he bent to help Alex up, the rain came down with a vengeance, soaking all of them.

Clara's mom was waiting at the door, "You're all wet! Come into the house and dry off," she said.

Inside they toweled themselves dry, changed into borrowed clothes, and then sipped mugs of hot chocolate around the kitchen table.

Clara went over to the window, wiped the moisture from the pane, and stood gazing outside with a worried frown. Over her shoulder, the girls stared at clouds, black as ravens, winging above the city, and the rain pelting down in glassy sheets. The constant pulse and crack of lightning and the booming bellow of thunder sounded like a rock band gone wild. The storm was beautiful and awesome in its fierceness, but they were too worried about Alba to enjoy it.

Finally, the rain tapped its farewell upon the roof, the growling of the thunder traveled on, and the sun slid over the horizon, transforming the neighborhood into a glistening crystal palace. The girls sprinted back to Alba, dodging fallen branches and roof shingles.

Sophie put her hands over her eyes as they approached the tree, "I'm afraid to look," she whispered.

"I'll go in front," Rose declared, thrusting her chin forward.

"Shut up," Clara said. "We'll all go together."

At first the girls didn't notice the twisted limb hanging like a cracked bone near the top of the tree, or the railings torn off one side of the tree house. They saw Alba standing straight and firm. They high-fived then did a victory lap around the tree, not caring about the mud oozing into their socks and splashing onto their clothes.

Mr. Datdan's car pulled up, and as he

came to a stop, he put his head out the window and called out, "Is everything okay?"

"Yes, thank goodness Alba survived the storm," Sarah said.

Mr. Datdan got out, and picking his way through the mud, looked up at the oak.

"That broken limb is dangerous. It could fall on the building, or worse yet on someone standing nearby," he sighed. "I'll have to call in a tree cutting expert to bring down a limb as thick as this one, and that's going to be expensive."

He left shaking his head and muttering, about the oak costing him more than his own kids.

Sophie's Story:
Two old trees, a scarlet oak and a loblolly pine, on the edge of our school's grounds went down in last night's storm. Lying uprooted on the ground with their roots sticking out like gigantic dinosaur nests, we could see the rot inside their trunks. It's sad that those big trees toppled, but they were ready to go, ready to become food for insects and fungi as they rot back into the earth. What if Alba Maizie had fallen? The death of our healthy oak tree would have been so sad. A small but important part of our world would have vanished. There's a busy life going on in that tree: crows, woodpeckers, robins, and nuthatches nest in its branches; red-tailed hawks and owls lurk on its topmost limbs, bats hide in its hole. Squirrel and chipmunks

scramble up its trunk for protection. The chattering, singing and calling of the birds and squirrels hanging out there, living there, finding meals there, is wonderful to hear. Children love to shelter in its shade, or climb its branches. It's the straightest and tallest white oak I've seen. Yet one man with a chainsaw or a bulldozer could so easily kill it. It's not just our tree I worry about. It's all those trees, felled one by one.

Thirteen

Vandals!

During the winter, the cold fingers of Jack Frost coated Alba's bare branches with a layer of ice crystals. The Sizzling Six visited their tree house less often. Now Alba seemed more alone and lonely than ever.

One Sunday afternoon, the girls strolled over to their tree, talking about the fun they had shared over the summer. They wondered if their dreamtime owl and their Evening Bat would return to Alba; they hoped that they would see these marvelous creatures when they spent the night in the tree house again.

As they approached the tree, Grace's eyes narrowed. "What's that on Alba's trunk?"

"Oh, no!" Sophie cried.

"Someone has carved their initials deep into it!" Sarah yelled.

Looking more closely, they saw a heart with the initials T.M. and J.S.

"Whoever did this is in for BIG trouble!" Rose shouted, waving her fist in the air.

They heard someone laughing in the tree house, and looked up to see the grinning faces of Tommy Minefield and his girlfriend Joanne Swain.

"How could you do something so cruel and unfair to a defenseless tree?" Sophie spat the words out.

"You think you're *so* special just because of your tree!" Tommy shouted back. He wore his head in a buzz cut, and they could see bumps on his scalp like a knobby gourd.

Like a swarm of angry hornets, the girls shinnied up the rope ladder. "Don't you understand that this tree doesn't belong to us?" Clara huffed, "It belongs to everyone." She yanked the edge of Tommy's shirt.

"Is that a fact?" Tommy sneered.

"Trees provide the oxygen that you breathe," Alex declared.

"Cutting into the tree will open it to infection and beetle infestation. Then it might rot and die!" Grace went on.

"Yeah, yeah, you're all just crazy enviruses!" Tommy scowled, twisting free of

Clara's grip.

"Huh? You mean environmentalists," Alex corrected him.

"It's so cool that our initials well be on the tree forever," Joanne giggled, tossing her long yellow ponytail.

Suddenly Jose Sanchez, a boy in Mrs. Green's class, was standing beneath Alba, looking up through glasses that pinched his nose. With an old backpack slung over his shoulder, wearing worn leather boots, faded jeans and a faded shirt, he looked sort of like a lumberjack.

He called out, "What's going on up there!"

That stopped Rose from almost smacking Tommy, instead she yelled, "Jose, did you help Tommy cut a scar in this tree?"

"Naw, I wouldn't do that! I like this tree."

Tommy scrambled down, and sneered at Jose. "So what're you going to do about it?" He kicked a stone and it narrowly missed hitting his girlfriend as she came down the ladder.

"Stop that!" Jose yelled, picking up a fallen stick.

"Catch me if you can, freak!" Tommy jeered, running off as fast as he could.

"Get him!" Rose yelled as Jose rushed after Tommy.

A very Tricky Situation Indeed:
How could they punish Tommy? How could they stop him from hurting trees without telling on him? Keep in mind that our tree wounds do not "heal" like skin injuries in mammals. We trees produce a callus—a hard outer layer of wood—that closes over our wounds. Large cuts usually do not close quickly, leaving us at risk being attacked by insects and bacteria.

Fourteen

Spring in the Air

After the long winter, the cycle of life started anew. Alba woke to drink in the spring rains and to draw energy from the sun. Leaves sprouted on every limb; the first leaves unfolded like delicate pink shells. Tiny yellow-green catkins, or male flowers, poked out. They grew long and dangled like earrings, swirling a mist of yellow pollen around Alba. This pollen floated on the wind to fertilize the small, red female flowers on other oaks, and after a few weeks they would become tiny acorns.

At dusk the air began flickering with fireflies, or lightning bugs. The male flashed his light in search of a female, who flashed her light back to him.

"If fireflies were big as dinosaurs, they would burn down the world!" Sarah fantasized.

"Their light is called bioluminescence," Alex explained.

"Yes, teacher," Rose teased.

The girls sneaked up behind the bugs and caught them in their cupped hands. They watched the green glow between their fingers then squealed because the fireflies tickled, making them open their fingers to let them fly off. They never gave the fireflies to their brothers who might hurt them.

Sometimes the girls just stood at Alba's base; they didn't hug it, but they leaned against it, looking straight up its rough trunk to its dizzying height, feeling the swaying movement of the limbs vibrate in their chests.

Back in class at Stone Middle, students trudged into Mrs. Green's fourth period class.

"Good afternoon, people. Your homework assignment was to read Chapter 9, covering food chains and food webs. Who can give examples how these webs maintain a balance in nature?"

Alex frowned; she didn't want to raise her hand because she hated being called a "know-it-all."

When no one answered, Mrs. Green stalked down the isle tapping desks with a long ruler.

"Let me start with an example. Do you know that fungi can invade the trunks and limbs of old or damaged trees where they are injured? The fungi soften the wood, and that enables beetles, wasp larvae, and carpenter ants to build tunnels in it to lay their eggs. When the eggs hatch into larvae they feed on the wood. In time this causes the tree to die, making space for new trees to grow.

"Now, look at the chart on page 102." When still not one student responded, she chided, "Wake up class! If no one can give examples you'll have to do an extra homework assignment."

At that point, several hands went up. Sarah gave the example of leaf-eating insects, like walking sticks, that can damage a tree if there are too many of them. She explained that when birds eat enough of these insects, they help to right the balance.

Francis Yen, who kept silkworms for pets, stood up next and described how caterpillars, when they grow in large numbers, can strip an oak tree of its leaves. However, there is a type of parasitic wasp that destroys caterpillars' eggs. If enough wasps eat their eggs, there will be fewer caterpillars, again serving to maintain the balance between the wasp and the caterpillar populations.

Mrs. Green looked pleased, but then she caught a movement out of the corner of her eye. Tommy Minefield was getting ready to throw a paper airplane at Jose Sanchez, and she pounced.

"Tommy, I know you're a keen fisherman, can you illustrate how earthworms help to maintain the balance in nature?"

Tommy crushed the paper airplane in his hand and shrugged.

"We're all waiting, Mr. Minefield."

"Uh, the balance, uh . . ."

"Anyone else care to explain? If not, it'll be your homework for tonight."

Sarah looked over at Alex and mouthed, *put up your hand, Alex.* Reluctantly Alex did so.

"Yes, Alex?"

"During the warm rainy season, earthworms stay above ground, but in winter they wriggle down in the earth to avoid freezing. So earthworms spend most of the winter below the surface where they fertilize and loosen the soil making it easier for new plant roots to grow in."

Thanks Alex, Jose mouthed.

Alex turned red and looked over at Sarah who gave her the thumbs up sign.

With this new understanding of how nature works, the students began to appreciate that each one of us is a part of life on this planet, and that every living thing is linked together in a huge web of life that includes humans—if one thread breaks, it weakens the whole.

Fifteen

Monday Surprises

On Monday morning the students trooped into Mrs. Green's class, wondering what surprise she had in store for them this time, but in place of Mrs. Green there was a substitute teacher. He informed them that Mrs. Green had broken her leg and would be back on Thursday.

The students felt bad for their teacher, and wondered what had caused the accident. They were also surprised to see that Tommy Minefield's right hand was bandaged, but he didn't seem to want to talk about it.

Around the dinner table that night, Sarah got the biggest surprise of all.

"You're not going to believe this, but someone cut down the damaged tree limb, and also repaired your tree house over the weekend," her dad said.

Sarah's mother put down her fork. "Who could have done us such a good deed?"

"Whoever did it, I'm thankful that they spared me from having to spend more money on that tree. To be honest I didn't have the cash to pay for it."

Sarah had her suspicions, but she wasn't going to say anything until she was sure. She e-mailed a message to the rest of the Sizzling Six, about the mysterious repair of Alba and the tree house.

A Small Question:
Who do you think made those repairs? You got that right.

Sixteen

Secret Agents

Almost an entire year had gone by since the girls first thought up the idea of building a tree house—and had actually succeeded in building it! Things had not progressed so well with the construction of Mr. Datdan's office during that school year.

To Mr. Datdan's frustration—and the secret delight of the Sizzling Six—construction of his office had to be delayed owing to slow work on the storm drains. Mr. Datdan had called the city council numerous times to try and hurry things up, only to be informed that the crew was tied up repairing roads washed out in the winter storm, and they would get to his project as soon as they could.

Shortly before construction was finally ready to begin, Mr. Datdan called Mr. Elder, an expert on trees from the U.S. Forestry Service, for advice on how to protect Alba. Since the girls worried about Alba's safety, he called Sarah on the cell phone to invite her friends to meet him at the oak.

They reached the construction site, panting for breath, to find Mr. Elder slowly circling Alba, measuring its trunk as he did so. Everything about him was tall and strong; in his green uniform, he almost looked like a tree himself. Mr. Datdan introduced the girls and he waved to them then went right on with his work.

When Mr. Elder had completed his walk around Alba, he gave a long, low whistle. "This sure is a strong, healthy oak, and should live for another hundred years, if you take good care of it," he said, as he stuck the measuring tape back in his pocket. "First, you need to place a fence around the tree. Bright plastic orange netting that you can buy at the hardware store will do. You can attach it to posts to make a barrier. It needs to extend beyond Alba's longest branches to ensure that its roots won't be injured. The fence will prevent dirt from being piled over the root system and smothering them," he said, spraying an orange circle around the tree with nontoxic spray paint.

"I will make sure that it's done," Mr. Datdan said.

The tree conservation man went on, "Roots are the most vital parts of a tree as they take up nutrients and water, and store energy for the tree. They also anchor it down to keep it from toppling over in a storm." He paused to look up at the tree again. "The barrier will help keep heavy machinery from running over the roots and packing the soil down so hard that oxygen and water can't soak to the roots. Also it will prevent machinery from breaking Alba's branches, or tearing its bark."

When building, at last, got underway, the Sizzling Six and their friends checked the fence at least once a week after the work crews had left, to make sure it hadn't been knocked down. They also inspected the area around Alba for chemicals that could poison its roots. They examined the ground to see if paintbrushes, cement, or other chemicals had been cleaned near the barrier, and that debris and waste had been hauled away, not burned or buried on the construction site. At first the crew kept the site clean, but as the pressure to finish the building by the deadline increased, the Sizzling Six noticed that they were becoming careless.

A Small Confession:
Some nasty chemicals did pool around my roots. Ugh! When the girls discovered the spill, they were determined to catch the wrongdoers.

The Six met in the tree house immediately after school to brainstorm ideas. Grace suggested they hide in the tree to spy on the cleanup crew. Sarah pointed out that they couldn't do that without being seen. The girls stared glumly up through the branches, until Rose slapped her knee and shouted, "I've got it!"

"So let's hear it," Grace said impatiently. Rose said that they should all climb into the tree in plain sight of the crew. About fifteen minutes later, five of them would come down and leave chatting loudly. One would stay behind. The odds were that the men were unlikely to notice that one of them was still in the tree. Everyone wanted to be the "spy," most of all Rose, the daredevil, so it had to be settled by tossing a coin.

Clara had the luck to win. *Or maybe it's my bad luck*, she thought nervously.

They put their plan into operation the very next day.

Late in the afternoon, Clara sat hunched in a fork of the tree, hardly daring to breathe, secretly observing the crew. It was almost quitting time, and the men were hurrying to finish the clean up, slopping paint thinner and paint around in their haste.

It seemed like hours, but within twenty minutes, all but one man had driven off. He was big, and had a nose like a scuffed up old sneaker that made the name "Scuffy" pop into her head.

Scuffy grunted as he washed off his boots with a hose, wetting a pile of almost empty cement bags, which should have been tossed in the dumpster. In the deep ruts made by tractor tires, the polluted water drained toward Alba. Clara slipped and nearly fell in her eagerness to snap photos of the crime scene. The man heard her yelp as she grabbed onto a branch to steady herself. Before he could look up, Clara swiftly hid the camera in her jacket pocket.

Craning his neck, Scuffy growled, "Go home! Kids like you should be doing their homework, not messing around." Picking up the wet cement bags, Scuffy hauled them off with a scowl.

Her knees weak with fear, Clara shinnied down. She didn't want him to become suspicious so she walked away slowly, although she wanted take off running. To her immense relief, Grace came whizzing down the street on her bike. Clara rushed over to her, jumped onto the handlebars and begged, "Get me out of here!"

As soon as she reached home, she called the Sizzling Six to come over to see the "hot evidence." When Mr. Datdan saw the photos he whistled in surprise and then said he would make sure it didn't happen again.

Another Problem Solved:
Thanks to the Sizzling Six, they caught the culprit in the act, and Mr. Datdan took care of him. I really couldn't wait for the workers to finish building and leave me in peace.

Seventeen

Who Did It?

When Mr. Datdan's office building was completed at the end of autumn, the girls could finally resume meeting in their tree house without being disturbed by the construction crews and their noisy machinery. Because the Sizzling Six had sketched, photographed, and kept notebooks while on their school field trips, they observed many things that they hadn't really noticed before. The way the light through and around the tree changed with the seasons: the hot, bright yellow light of summer, the cold, misty gray of winter, the delicate, fresh green of spring, and the brilliant red and gold of fall. The sounds were different, too; the drumming of a rainstorm in summer; the trumpeting of winds gusting through the bare trees in winter; the pattering of a shower and the whispering of breezes playing around the leaves in spring; the dry swishing of leaves twirling to the ground in fall. The texture of the leaves also felt different to the touch; bendable in summer, brittle in the winter, soft in spring, leathery in fall.

"I've been wondering about who could have repaired Alba's broken branch and our tree house," Sarah said.

"I've got my suspects," Grace replied.

"Who do you think did it?" Rose challenged her.

"Mrs. Green and Tommy."

The others gasped in disbelief.

"Get serious, Grace! How can you prove it?" Clara asked.

"First, Mrs. Green broke her leg right after the storm cracked one of Alba's branches, and right after that we found out someone repaired it. Second, Tommy injured his hand at the same time the tree house was repaired and the same time Mrs. Green broke her leg. Third, neither of them wanted to talk about how they got hurt."

"I see what you're getting at, but still we can't know for sure," Clara said.

"I guess not, but I'm going to think of a way to find out!" Grace said.

The girls shook their heads, knowing Grace might think up something that could get them into trouble.

To their surprise Sophie said, "Wait! I just had an idea that might help to solve the mystery." She tapped the side of her head.

"Including how the green streaks got into Mrs. Green's hair?" Rose asked.

"Don't push our luck," Alex retorted.

"Okay, so here's my plan," Sophie said.

A week after her accident, Mrs. Green limped briskly into her fourth period class on crutches. She didn't look feeble or wobbly; she looked determined. The green streaks in her hair were more visible than ever, and her cleanly scrubbed skin glowed. As she picked up the textbook on her desk she noticed a green envelope with her name on it. She frowned, then reached over and opened it. When she finished reading the card, decorated with a border of oak leaves, she looked up. Her eyes flickered around the class, and came to rest on Alex. Mrs. Green looked at her with raised eyebrows.

"May I say something, Mrs. Green?"

"Only if it's important."

"On behalf on all the students we want to thank you for helping us adopt Alba, and for taking us on all those field trips. Also thank you for repairing the broken tree branch, we're sorry you broke your leg doing it."

The whole class rose, cheering and clapping. For once, Mrs. Green was at a loss for words, she looked as if she was trying to blink away tears.

After the students settled down, she cleared her throat and said, "It was my pleasure. You also should thank Tommy Minefield, too, for repairing the tree house."

Tommy turned red; he hated to have his reputation as a bully spoiled by praise from a teacher. But when the students started cheering him, he couldn't stop himself from breaking into a grin.

"Enough, people. From now on I expect each one of you to return the favor by working hard and earning good grades."

Eighteen

Hatching New Adventures

"You know I've been thinking about those two old trees that toppled in the storm," Grace said.

"I wish they were still there." Sarah had a dreamy, far away look in her eyes.

"Instead of dreaming, why don't we do something about it?" Rose challenged her.

"Yeah, we proved that the Sizzling Six *can* make it happen if they are determined enough!" Grace beamed.

"Yeah, the Sizzling Six sure showed that grumpy old Mr. Prickles what we can do!" Clara declared.

"So how about we take on the project Mrs. Green suggested? You know, the one about getting Alba selected as a Landmark Tree?" Alex asked.

"Mr. Birch talked about Alba being honored as a Historic Tree," Sophie added. "That really sounded interesting."

"Whoa, use your common sense, we can't take on all three projects at once," Clara cautioned.

"So, let's take a vote. First, who agrees to take on a new mission?" Sophie wanted to know.

"Come on! We don't need to vote, you know we're always ready for action!" Grace declared.

"Just to be fair," Sophie said, looking at her friends, "let's vote on which one to do first. A show of hands for planting new trees on our school's grounds?"

Five hands shot up, only Grace kept her hand stubbornly at her side. Everyone looked disapprovingly at her, but she grinned back. Just as Rose was about to chew her out, Grace giggled and said, "Just kidding."

"Okay, then it's settled. After we complete that project, with the help of our parents, teachers and kids at Stone Middle, we'll start working on the Landmark Tree. When that's done we'll get going on the Historic Tree project," Alex said.

"Give me five!" Grace held out her hand and the others took turns slapping her palm.

Nineteen

Not Quite So Happily Ever After

Now Alba rises high above the neighborhood like a beacon. It spreads shade over those who come to picnic or to play around it. Birds nest in its branches, insects feed on its leaves and bark, wildlife scamper up its trunk for protection and eat its acorns for nourishment. School children come to marvel at it, to study it, and to daydream in the tree house beneath its sheltering branches. Even when they come alone, they never feel lonely because Alba is a part of nature and they are a part of it, too.

A Small Sad Note:
The forest around me is gone. I stand alone, yet I am a bridge from the man-made city to the wilder world in the fields and woods beyond. The children care about me, and have come to appreciate nature through me. I hope to keep growing strong and tall for generations of children to come.

About The Author

Claire Datnow is the author of biographies for young adults, *Edwin Hubble Discoverer of Galaxies*, and *American Science Fiction and Fantasy Writers*. A teacher of gifted students, she has a keen interest in preserving the natural environment and received the Blanche Dean Award for Outstanding Nature Education, from the Alabama Conservancy. She enjoys traveling to faraway places, designing nature trails, and taking long walks with her granddaughters.

22583176R00052

Made in the USA
Charleston, SC
28 September 2013